Why Don't Big Boys Cry?

Written by Derrick Malone Jr.
Illustrated by Yasmeen Gutierrez

To request permissions, contact the publisher at
normallyunstable@gmail.com

Hardcover: ISBN 978-1-7364248-0-3

First hardcover edition February 2021
Edited by Joel Gunderson
Illustrated by Yasmeen Gutierrez
Printed in the United States of America

To those whose tears will be accompanied by a smile - pain is only temporary.

This is Koby. Koby is about your age. He may be a year older or a year younger, but, for the most part, Koby is just like you.

He has two friends - Carl and Carla -, and they do everything together. Whether it's raining or the sun is shining, you'll find the three of them playing outside or debating who's the strongest superhero around.

When it's time to learn, they like to sit side by side, reading their books together.

But most importantly, if one of them is having a bad day, the others are around to lend helping hands.

In his mind, Koby's life was picture perfect, until one day, it all came crashing down.
While he was playing in the hallway outside his parents' bedroom, he overheard the news. With his ear pressed against the door, Koby heard his mother whispering to his father.

home Sweet home
"So, it's official, then -- We have to move.."
Koby's mother had taken a new job many miles away. Koby now had to say goodbye to his friends and the only life he has ever known. He had to say goodbye to it all. "I hope Koby takes it well."

Koby would have to say goodbye to his favorite tree, which provided him
shade on those hot summer days.

Goodbye to the corner wall in his room, which he used to track his height, from a tiny toddler to the brilliant boy he was today.

Worst of all, he had to say goodbye to Carl and Carla.
Sitting in his room, he promised them they'd be best friends forever.

Koby was sad, and held back tears because, in his mind, big boys don't cry.
But why?

Koby's first week at his new school didn't go as well as he hoped it would. On his first day, he missed the morning bus.

Unfortunately for Koby, as the days passed on,
nothing seemed to get easier. He missed
his old life more and more.

Although he was sad, he never let anyone see him cry. He bottled up the tears, tucked them away deep inside his body, and never let them out. Because, in his mind, big boys don't cry.

But why?

Sept
08

After every school day, once the final bell rang, Koby grabbed his belongings and sprinted home.

Once home, he would hide in the treehouse in his backyard, which Koby's father built when they first moved into the neighborhood.

They thought it would help ease the transition. As Koby would call it, 'The Fort', would be a place where friendships were created.

It would be a place for cookies and milk, stories, and sleepovers.
But as time wore on and friendships became harder to make, The Fort became a safe, quiet place for Koby to escape, think, and reflect.

One evening. As dinnertime approached, Koby's mom started wondering where her son was.
"Koby? Koby, where are you?" she yelled, searching for him high and low.

Soon she spotted him up in The Fort and whispered to Koby's dad, "He's right here."

"He seems upset, maybe you should talk to him?" she continued. Dad nodded in agreement.

Don't cry. Don't do it.

"Is everything okay?" Koby's father asked.

"I don't know. I'm fine, I guess," Koby answered.

"'I don't know' is not acceptable, Koby. Talk to me. Your eyes are red; have you been crying?"

"No, I haven't been crying," Koby lied. For the first time in forever, he had let the tears fall, but it hadn't made him feel any better.

"I just miss our old home. I miss my old friends. My old life. And I promise I wasn't crying, dad. I'm a big boy. Big boys don't cry."

"Big boys don't cry??"

Koby's father repeated, concerned at what he had heard, "Where did you learn that?"

[Has a flashback]

"I'm not quite sure when I first heard it.

Maybe on TV. Or from Uncle Jimmy," Koby says.

"Or maybe I learned it at the barbershop?

I can't remember.

"Let me tell you something, Koby - change can be scary and unexpected, and that's why there's absolutely nothing wrong with crying. I cried today."

"YOU cried?" Koby asked, his eyes widening. He was shocked. "But, you're so big and strong... how could you cry?"

"Well, son, big boys DO cry - and here's why...

"Being vulnerable is what makes you a big boy. A big boy can cry alone,
with family and friends, or even around strangers - and that
wouldn't make you any less strong," his dad said.
"Crying is healthy, because afterward, you may feel a
huge weight being lifted off of your shoulders."

At this moment, Koby began to change his beliefs about crying.

"Because . . ." his dad continued, "Big boys DO get Knocked down. They wipe away their tears and continue fighting for what's right.

Big boys DO find ways to be kind, generous, and respectful to everyone. Big boys DO comfort others in their time of need. Big boys DO find strength in showing emotion."

Koby's dad slid in closer and wrapped his right arm around the boy's shoulder, pulling him in tight.

"Now that, son, is what it means to be a big boy. Does that make sense? "

"Yes," Koby replied, "it does."

"So," his dad continued, "let me ask you. Is it wrong to cry because you stubbed your toes?"

"No," Koby replies.

"Is it wrong to cry because of your food being too spicy?" Koby lets out a small laugh, then looks up at his dad.

"No, it's not wrong."

The next week at school started just as all of the others had. Koby was picked last on the soccer field - but this time, he was excited to play. As Koby was running across the field, he collided with a kid from the opposite team during the game.

As both kids tumbled to the ground, Koby scraped his knee. The game stopped, and everyone stared at Koby to see what he was going to do.

A few tears fell from his eyes, but he wiped them away. He brushed himself off and stayed in the game

With two minutes left, Koby scored the winning goal! Everyone was so excited - and cheered and celebrated with him. It was the start of his new life that he had been waiting for.

Now, Koby has another reason to shed tears. Tears of joy.

Because he's a big boy, and big boys do cry.

17
04
11
07

Derrick Malone Jr. studied Journalism & Communications at the University of Oregon, where he played NCAA Division-1 Football from 2010 - 2014. In the year 2015, Derrick partnered with the university to tell the story of his struggles with mental health, which has since sparked a passion for writing, and helping others in similar situations.

Malone Jr. has published numerous articles for The Oregonian newspaper and has self-published two books. He continues to be a passionate mental health advocate, as well as a public speaker, where he has helped spread the word on mental health to corporations and schools, both K-12 and higher education institutions. His goal is to reduce the stigma around the conversation of mental health.

CPSIA information can be obtained
at www.ICGtesting.com
Printed in the USA
BVHW052206230421
605720BV00002B/58

* 9 7 8 1 7 3 6 4 2 4 8 0 3 *